D0508070

For my Michael, with all my love xx ~ CF

For our friend Pete. A reminder, keep your hair on! ~ SH and PL

Bloomsbury Publishing, London, Oxford, New York, New Delhi and Sydney

First published in Great Britain in 2017 by Bloomsbury Publishing Plc
50 Bedford Square, London WC1B 3DP

www.bloomsbury.com

BLOOMSBURY is a registered trademark of Bloomsbury Publishing Plc

Text copyright © Claire Freedman 2017
Illustrations copyright © Sue Hendra 2017
The moral rights of the author and illustrator have been asserted

A CIP catalogue record of this book is available from the British Library

ISBN 978 1 4088 6716 7 (HB)
ISBN 978 1 4088 6717 4 (PB)
ISBN 978 1 4088 6715 0 (eBook)

All papers used by Bloomsbury Publishing are natural, recyclable products made
from wood grown in well managed forests. The manufacturing processes
conform to the environmental regulations of the country of origin

Printed in China by Leo Paper Products, Heshan, Guangdong

1 3 5 7 9 10 8 6 4 2

SCARY HAIRY PARTY!

Claire Freedman

Illustrated by Sue Hendra
and Paul Linnet

BLOOMSBURY
LONDON OXFORD NEW YORK NEW DELHI SYDNEY

You're invited to a party —
what fun! Hip, hip, hooray!

All Monster's friends are dressing up
in quite their party best.

Well, except for little Mumu —
HE wants to wear his vest!

WOW! Outside Raymond's hair salon
the queue goes on FOREVER.

As everybody wants to get
the nicest hairdo EVER!

Belle's first. She's SO excited
as she sits on Raymond's chair.

But too much hairspray in the air
makes Belle's hair stick like glue.

"It's awful!" snuffles little Belle.
"What am I going to do?"

Next Leo's mane is crimped and primped.
Then hair gelled — just a dab.

"Make it GRRR-REAT!" growls Leo.
"I need to look just FAB!"

Poor Leo's feeling quite upset,
"This isn't PARTY hair!"

Another **big** disaster —
Raymond muddles up the dyes.

And Finlay, Ron and Mumu get a **SCARY** big surprise.

With **rainbow** dye and **frizzy** perms,
mad hair and **gloopy goo**...

All Monster's friends are in a tizz,
"What are WE going to do?"

But look who's come to find them
with a smile upon her face . . .

"My party's starting now," she calls.
"Quick — over to my place!"

"Come in, come in!" says Monster.
"This is going to be such fun . . .

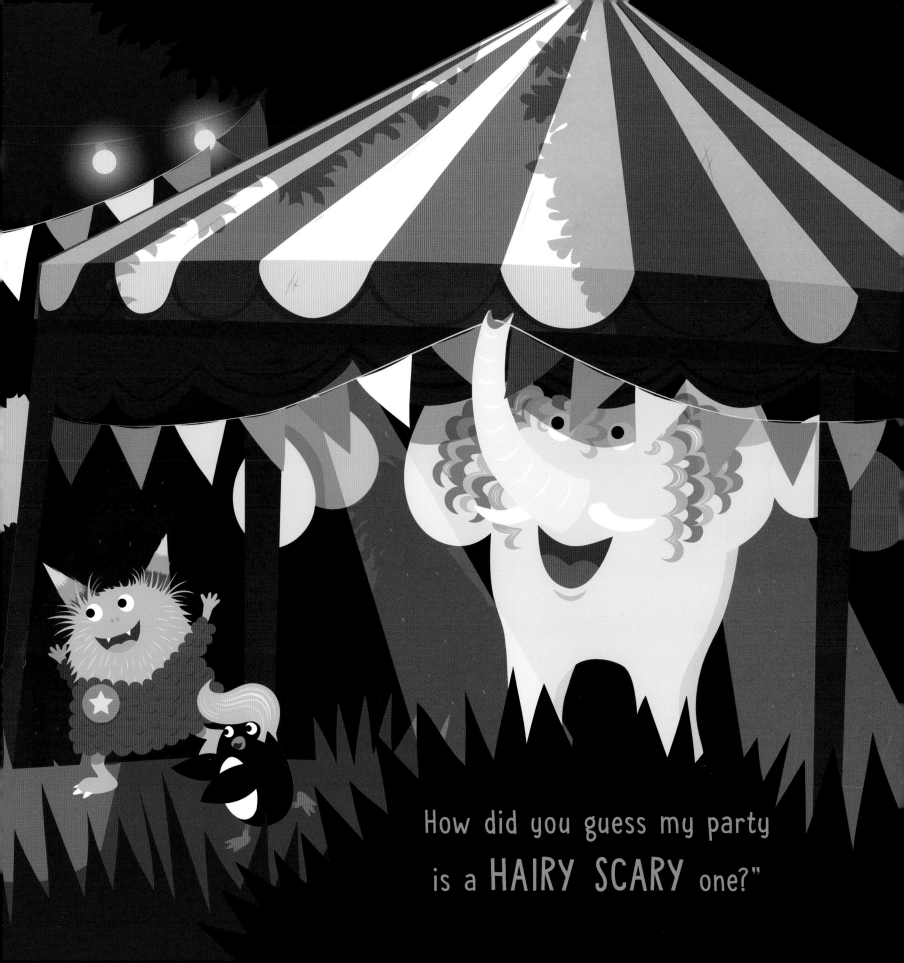

How did you guess my party
is a HAIRY SCARY one?"

"Oh, Raymond!" cheer the happy friends.
"You are so VERY clever!

We think this party has to be
the BESTEST party EVER!"